Where can you row a boat
and birdwatch?

How do you know whether you're
on the East or the West Side,
once you're inside the Park?

If you want to breakdance,
where's a good spot?

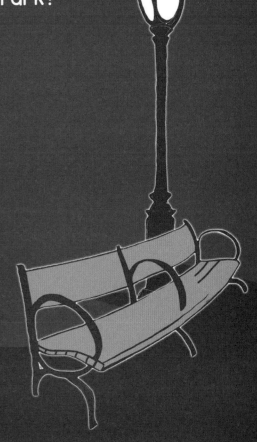

THE CENTRAL PARK LOST MITTEN PARTY

By Fran Quittel

For all those who delight in urban public parks.

Copyright © 2018 by Fran Quittel / text and illustrations

ISBN 13: 978-1-58790-446-2
ISBN 10: 1-58790-446-2
Library of Congress Catalog Number: 2018946414

Summary: Imaginative tale allowing everything we lose to celebrate a wondrous party in Central Park before magically returning home. Includes full-color illustrations, historical notes, detailed bibliography, educational material, suggested Park activities.

Audience: Ages 6 to 12 | K – Grade 7 | parents | local NY | visitors | worldwide friends of Central Park and urban parks |

For further information or to order:
info@centralparklostmittenparty.com
www.centralparklostmittenparty.com

Published by GINGERSPICE PRESS, *an imprint of Regent Press*

REGENT PRESS
Berkeley, California
www.regentpress.net
regentpress@mindspring.com
510-845-1196

Printed by We SP Corp., Seoul, Korea
Production Date   2018-06-05
Plant & Location   Printed in South Korea
Job / Batch #   81308

Where do your lost mittens and gloves go in New York City?

To dance the night away in the heart of Central Park, of course!

Perhaps as you read *The Central Park Lost Mitten Party*, you will recognize some of the Park's many exquisite locations. These include the Delacorte Clock and *Alice in Wonderland* statue, Bethesda Fountain, Terrace and Arcade, the Carousel, Greywacke Arch, Belvedere Castle, Paul Manship's *Group of Bears*, the Naumburg Bandshell, the World's Fair style cast iron bench, Bow Bridge, and the Henry Bacon lamp post.

The designs on the *Lost Mitten Party* mittens and gloves reference some of the many beautiful and unique motifs of Central Park's balustrades, columns, bridges and arches. The hats on the mittens, gloves and socks are based on hats worn by Radio City Rockettes.

Enjoy!

One morning near Central Park's
Fountains and streams,
A little girl slept
Dreaming teddy bear dreams.

1

As her Mommy called softly, "Wake up, sleepyhead!
It's time for school, Molly. Let's get out of bed."

"It's cold and it's rainy, and today you can wear
Your big rubber boots and a hat on your hair,
A scarf just for winter, a snowsuit that laughs,
And earmuffs and mittens, painted with big giraffes!
These mittens are magic, my Molly will see,
They're warm, cozy, comfy, and snug as can be."

And when school was over, and Molly came home,
She held just one mitten, one mitten alone.

"Don't worry, my sweetheart," Mommy said with a smile,
"We'll find it tomorrow or after a while.
So good night and sweet dreams, though your mitten may roam,
When you wake up tomorrow, we might find that it's home."

And later that night, with stars lighting their way,
All the lost mittens hopped out to play.

Deep inside Central Park,
They danced under the stars,
All those lost mittens, lost toys, dolls, and scarves.

All colors and sizes,
Some wool, and some leather,
They clapped, skipped and jumped,
And danced all together!

Umbrellas popped open.
Bears sang songs and marches.

10

The shoes were so happy,
They danced with galoshes.

And when it was midnight, and one, two, and three,
A wizard came out and stood calm as can be.

He clapped his hands twice,
And then looked high and low,
As all the lost mittens
Danced to and fro.

They leaped in the air and soon started to fly,
Towards home, towards school, way up there in the sky.

13

Once again with his hands, he clapped one, two, and three,
And all the lost mittens were safe as can be!

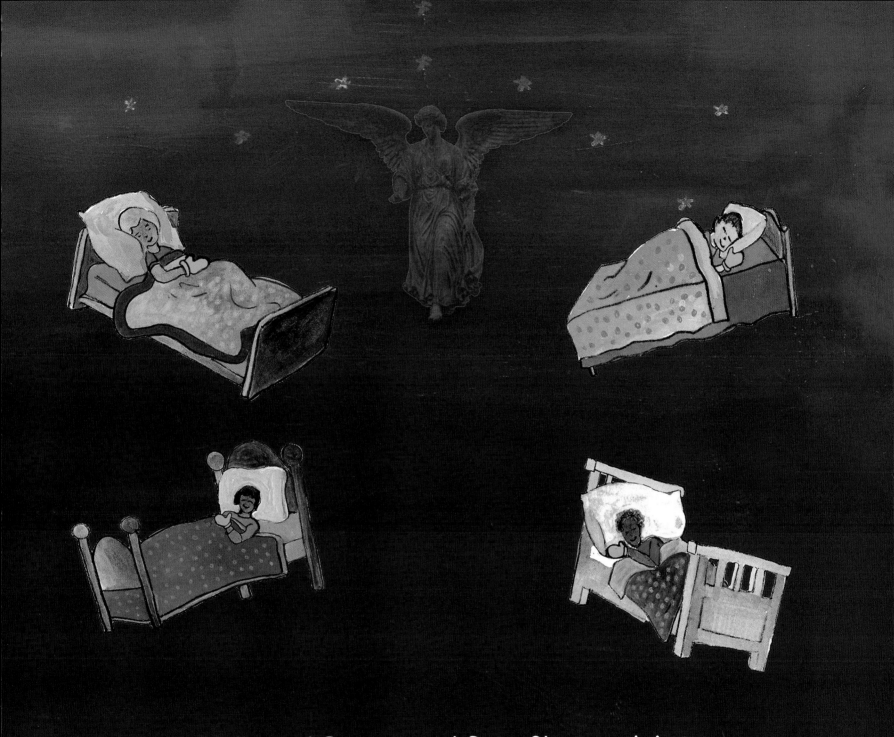

Back with Molly and Bonnie, and Dan, Chris and Artie,
All those lost mittens at the Central Park party
Were now home safe and sound, back with Jennie and Blair,
All the lost mittens were snug as a bear!

So whenever you see a lost mitten or glove,
Lost train, sock, or doll—or heavens above—
A shoe or lost rabbit, an umbrella or cap,
A lunch box or sweater or even a hat,

Remember at midnight, when the moon is quite dark,
All the lost mittens deep inside Central Park,
Are singing and laughing, as they dance and they play,

Then all those lost mittens, the very next day,
Fly home to their owners, on magic balloons,
All the lost mittens fly under the moon,
Back to Molly and Bonnie, and Dan, Chris and Artie,
After one magic night at the Central Park party.

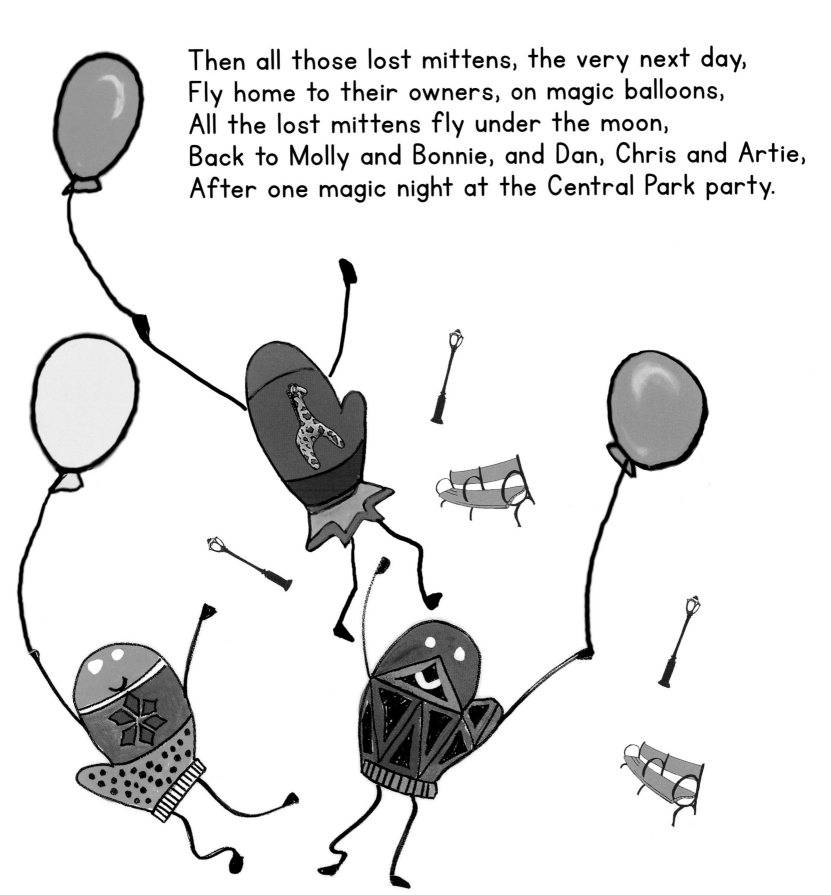

19

PS (for grownups)

And when you are grown up with hurry-up days,
Warm memories of pumpkins and jingle bell sleighs,
Fly you high over stars, all aglow in the dark,
To the lost mitten party deep inside Central Park,

Where your childhood treasures, toy ponies, and trains,
Come to life once again in the mitten parade.

And forever and always, whether nearby or far,
Whether grownup or child, whoever you are,

Whatever you lose in the rush of the day,
Comes to Central Park's meadows to run, skate, and play.

Over fountains and castles, all sail with delight,
As the carousel spins through the white winter night.

And then in the morning, this secret comes true,
As your precious treasures fly home again too.

Central Park Benches

The Park's over 9,000 benches are designed in four main styles: settee, rustic, wood-and-concrete, and the Robert Moses "hoop" arm cast iron bench, also known as the "World's Fair Bench". Special benches include the "Whisper Bench" in the Shakespeare Garden, and the Andrew Haswell Green Bench, at the north end of the Park, commemorating the "Father of Greater New York", whose achievements include bringing all five boroughs together to form one big city. Over 4,000 benches have been dedicated through the Central Park Conservancy's Women's Committee Adopt-A-Bench program.

New York City's Central Park

Central Park, the first urban landscaped park in the United States, was originally established by the New York State Legislature in 1853. The Park runs two and one-half miles north to south, from 59th to 110th Streets, and, east to west, one-half mile wide, from Fifth Avenue to Central Park West.

In 1857, landscape architect Frederick Law Olmsted (1822–1903), born in Hartford, Connecticut, became Central Park's first superintendent. He and British-American architect and landscape designer, Calvert Vaux (1824–1895), created their 1858 Greensward plan, which was chosen over thirty-two other submissions. Amazingly, both men's lives ended quite sadly. In 1895, Vaux drowned in Brooklyn, and Olmsted was committed with dementia to residential care in Massachusetts, where he died in 1903.

Central Park Lamp Posts and Numbering System

Henry Bacon (1866–1924), the Beaux-Arts architect who designed the Lincoln Memorial, was also responsible for the design of the Park's approximately 1,600 cast iron lamp posts in about 1907. With their botanical forms of leaves, buds and seeds, each lamp ends with an acorn at the top. In 1981, new cast aluminum luminaires from Kent Bloomer Studios in New Haven, Connecticut were designed to sit on top of Henry Bacon's original lamp posts.

Looking for your location in the Park? Look at the four-number system plaque on each lamp post. The first two numbers refer to the street. The second two numbers will end "even" (for the East Side), and "odd," for the West.

Greywacke Arch

Central Park's Conservancy currently counts 39 bridges and arches in the Park.

Greywacke Arch is located near the Metropolitan Museum of Art. It is one of many collaborations in the Park between Calvert Vaux and British-born architect, musician and linguist, Jacob Wrey Mould (1825–1886).

This particular arch is named for the type of Hudson River Valley sandstone used to build it, and its Moorish style celebrates Jacob Wrey Mould's studies at the Alhambra Palace in Granada, Spain.

Sheep Meadow

Sheep Meadow was originally the largest meadow in the Park. Sheep really did graze there from 1864 until 1934, eating the grass, fertilizing the lawn, and stopping traffic while crossing the road with their shepherd. Sheep Meadow is located on the west side of the Park, from 66th to 69th Streets.

Bethesda Terrace and Fountain

Bethesda Terrace and Fountain are located at 72nd Street Cross Drive. This central area, with its majestic staircases, was specified in the Park's original Greensward plan and executed by Calvert Vaux and Jacob Wrey Mould. It is an ideal spot to watch performances, visitors, row boats, and wedding photography.

The Angel of the Waters Sculpture

On top of Bethesda Fountain is the bronze, eight-foot Neoclassical *Angel of the Waters* sculpture, which was dedicated in 1873. This sculpture is by Emma Stebbins, who is considered to be the first woman to receive a major art commission in New York City. (Her brother, Henry Stebbins, was, at the time, president of the Central Park Board of Commissioners.) The Angel holds a lily in her left hand and steps forward with her left foot. Underneath the Angel are four cherubs representing Temperance, Purity, Health and Peace. The Central Park Conservancy restored the fountain in the 1980's.

Bethesda Terrace Arcade and Minton Ceiling

Restored in 2007, Bethesda Terrace Arcade's rare Minton-tile ceiling features 49 panels, each with 324 tiles. Designed in the mid-1860s by Calvert Vaux and Jacob Wrey Mould, the tiles were manufactured by the Minton Company of Stoke-on-Trent, England.

Paul Manship's Group of Bears

Central Park has many commemorative locations, among them, the Pat Hoffman Friedman Memorial Playground, which includes Paul Manship's bronze sculpture of three bears on a circular pedestal. The sculpture and the playground are both gifts of Samuel N. Friedman, in memory of his wife, Pat. The sculpture, cast in 1960, was unveiled in 1990 when the playground, located at East 79th Street, was dedicated.

The Naumburg Bandshell

The popularity of Central Park's concerts and the musical passion of Central Park architect Jacob Wrey Mould led to the construction of the first wooden and cast iron Mould Bandstand in 1862. New York City merchant, banker, and philanthropist, Elkan Naumburg (1835–1924), replaced the Mould Bandstand in 1923. In 1993, the Coalition to Save the Naumburg Bandshell won a legal victory to preserve this neoclassical structure. Dance, skate, sit, or listen to music at this location just south of Bethesda Terrace between 66th and 72nd Streets.

The Delacorte Clock

Located near the Children's Zoo and Wildlife Center, the Delacorte Clock was created in 1965, and donated by publisher George Delacorte, the founder of Dell Publishing (now owned by Random House). Sculptor Andrea Spadini created the six animals which dance below the clock every hour and half hour between 8 am and 6 pm, after the monkeys above the clock finish hitting the bell. The animals usually dance to the music of a glockenspiel, which chimes out a digitally programmed score of 32 nursery rhymes or, at holiday times, Christmas songs.

Belvedere Castle

Designed by Frederick Olmsted, Calvert Vaux, and Jacob Wrey Mould after their reappointment to oversee the Park's construction in 1865, Belvedere Castle (or beautiful view) is one of the highest points of the Park. The Castle, located at 79th Street, was originally built as a lookout structure without enclosed windows in 1869.

Since 1919, it is the home of National Weather Service equipment, giving us this familiar tagline: "The temperature in Central Park." The Castle was renovated as a Nature Center in 1983, and is scheduled for more renovations in 2018.

The Alice in Wonderland Statue

Also funded by publisher and philanthropist George Delacorte, Central Park's *Alice in Wonderland* statue, erected in 1959, commemorates Mr. Delacorte's first wife, Margarita, who loved reading Lewis Carroll's *Alice's Adventures in Wonderland* to their children. The sculpture, located at 76th Street and Fifth Avenue, near Conservatory Lake, was cast by Modern Art Foundry in Long Island City, Queens. It is based on the original illustrations of Sir John Tenniel, which brought Lewis Carroll's White Rabbit, Mad Hatter, Dormouse, Cheshire Cat, and, of course, Alice, to life. The figure of Alice is based on Sir John's daughter, Donna.

Bow Bridge

Crossing Central Park Lake, Bow Bridge, the longest bridge in the Park, was built in 1862. It is shaped like an archer's bow, and is again the work of Calvert Vaux and Jacob Wrey Mould. The bridge's ironwork was made by Janes, Kirtland & Co., the Bronx-based foundry which also created the cast iron Washington, DC Capitol dome and the railings of the Brooklyn Bridge.

The Friedsam Memorial Carousel

Located near the South end of the Park at 65th Street, Central Park's fourth Carousel's official name recognizes a gift from the foundation of the late philanthropist Colonel Michael Friedsam, who became the president of Fifth Avenue department store, B. Altman, in 1913.

The original Carousel was built in 1871. Until 1912, when it was motorized, it was turned by a live mule or horse, which was stationed underneath the platform and responded to the operator's tapped cue. After the next two carousels burned down, the Parks Department searched for a replacement, eventually locating a vintage carousel in an old BMT trolley terminal in Coney Island. The current Carousel was built in Brooklyn in 1908 by the Artistic Caroussel [sic] Manufacturers, where expert carvers Sol Stein and Harry Goldstein, Yiddish-speaking Russian immigrants, opened their own shop in 1906. Sol carved the heads and legs of the extra-large horses and Harry, the bodies. A Ruth und Sohn band organ from Germany supplies the music. The Carousel was restored by the Conservancy in 1990.

Located in the Park's famed Children's District, Playmates Arch connects the Carousel to the Dairy. In the past, the Dairy supplied fresh milk to children. It is now a visitor center and gift shop.

Bibliography

The Bridges of Central Park, Authors: Jennifer C. Spiegler and Paul M. Gaykowski, Arcadia Publishing, 2006.

Central Park, An American Masterpiece, A Comprehensive History of the Nation's First Urban Park, Author: Sara Cedar Miller, Abrams Books, 2003.

Central Park Then and Now, Author: Marcia Reiss, Pavilion, 2015.

Creating Central Park, Author: Morrison H. Hecksher, Metropolitan Museum of Art, 2008, second printing, 2011.

Gilded Lions and Jeweled Horses: The Synagogue to the Carousel, Catalog of the 2007 – 2008 American Folk Art Museum exhibit, Guest Curator: Murray Zimiles. Catalog co-publishers: The American Folk Art Museum with Brandeis University Press, 2007.

The Park and the People: A History of Central Park, Authors: Roy Rosenzweig and Elizabeth Blackmar, Cornell University Press, 1992, reprinted 1998.

Saving Central Park, A History and a Memoir, Author: Elizabeth Barlow Rogers, Knopf Publishing Group, 2018.

Seeing Central Park: The Official Guide to the World's Greatest Urban Park, Author: Sara Cedar Miller, Abrams Books, 2009.

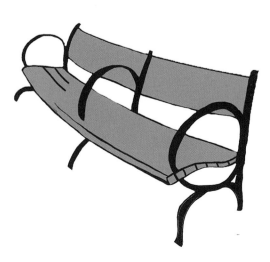

Explore the Park

To Visit

Central Park has five visitor centers and offers many tours and activities delighting children and adults, whether out-of-town visitors or life-long New York residents. Visiting the Park is free, as are many events and activities.

The Central Park Conservancy, which manages the Park, also offers professional programs and institutes. Conservancy fundraising contributes 75% of the Park's annual budget. Visit www.centralparknyc.org

The Official Website of the New York City Department of Parks & Recreation also offers detailed information about the Park. Visit www.nycgovparks.org/parks/central-park

Find other visitor information at: www.nycgo.com, www.iloveny.com, and www.centralpark.com

More Resources

For a history of the Park, Central Park, A Research Guide:
www.centralparknyc.org/assets/pdfs/institute/Central-Park-Conservancy-Research-Guide.pdf

For a variety of information about Central Park locations and the people who created them:
https://en.wikipedia.org/wiki/Central_Park

For the history of the Naumburg Bandshell and to listen to concerts:
www.naumburgconcerts.org

For the City Parks Foundation's annual SummerStage in Central Park concert series:
https://cityparksfoundation.org/summerstage/

To inspire parks and gardens throughout New York City, visit New York Restoration Project, www.nyrp.org, and, for open spaces throughout the country, the Trust for Public Land, www.tpl.org

Treasures Nearby

West Side:

Columbus Circle (59th Street, Central Park West)
Museum of Arts and Design
Lincoln Center for the Performing Arts
The Juilliard School
The American Folk Art Museum
The N.Y. Historical Society
The DiMenna Children's History Museum
The American Museum of Natural History
The Children's Museum of Manhattan
The Central Park West Historic District

Museum Mile on the East Side:

Metropolitan Museum of Art
Neue Galerie New York
The Solomon R. Guggenheim Museum
Cooper Hewitt, National Design Museum
The Jewish Museum
El Museo del Barrio
The Museum of the City of New York

More Fun

Wear your fancy hat

Celebrate the Central Park Conservancy and wear your fancy hat to the Annual Frederick Law Olmsted Awards Luncheon and Hat Gala.

Go to the Zoo

Visit snow monkeys, penguins, red pandas, sea lions, and grizzly bears.

Be inspired by a famous author

Write poetry, a song, a novel, or maybe a play along Central Park Mall's Literary Walk with these authors: Englishman William Shakespeare, Scotsmen Robert Burns and Sir Walter Scott, and American, Fitz-Greene Halleck.

Ice skate in winter, play tennis in spring

In winter, ice skate at Wollman Rink at the Park's south end, or Lasker Rink, at the north. From April to November, play tennis at one of the Park's thirty courts.

Take a special tour

Rent a bike, visit the locations of famous films, create an art project, or ride a horse drawn carriage.

Run, jump, skip and play

Do yoga, walk, run, or bike for charity, or ride high on the swings in one of Central Park's twenty-one playgrounds.

Learn to dance

In summer months, enjoy Argentine Tango lessons on Saturdays, and the Harlem Meer Performance Festival on Sundays.

Take a nap

Except when closed after 1 a.m., over 9,000 benches, plus meadows, lawns, and hills are readily available.

Author's Note

The original inspiration for *The Central Park Lost Mitten Party* came from an evening out with my beloved "almost aunt", Florence Belsky. Florence was one of the very first women to be appointed Special Referee of the New York Supreme Court. She was also an unwavering, lifelong champion of public education, Hunter College, Brooklyn College Law School, the New York Public Library, the Metropolitan Museum of Art, the opera, the arts, and all that New York has to offer. "When are you coming to New York?" was her special mantra to entice friends worldwide to visit her favorite hometown.

One evening, as we attended a performance at the Brooklyn Academy of Music, Florence suddenly realized that she had dropped one glove. "Don't worry about that glove," I said to console her. "It's in Central Park having a party!" "Now that's all right in a story for children," attorney Florence responded, never dreaming that her reply might inspire a magical fantasy where misplaced cold weather paraphernalia happily danced the night away in the heart of the City.

Perhaps as you read *The Central Park Lost Mitten Party*, you will experience the transformative effect of a snug embrace and the gift of imagination to soothe life's unexpected "bumps in the road" that Florence also felt that very first night. "I can't begin to tell you how amazed and thrilled I am," Florence wrote me. "Much love."

Do You Know

How many bridges and arches are there in Central Park?

Originally, Central Park had 35 bridges. The official count is now 39.

Were there ever really sheep in Sheep Meadow?

Yes, until the Depression in 1934.

Where in the Park can you row boats and birdwatch?

You can dine, birdwatch, or rent a boat near Bethesda Fountain and Terrace. The Central Park (or Loeb) Boathouse restaurant and the boat rental facility both sit at the Lake's east end.

How do you know whether you're on the East Side or the West Side once you're inside the Park?

The first two numbers of the plate on each lamp post tell you the street. If the number ends "odd", you're on the West Side, if even, on the East.

If you want to breakdance, where's a good spot?

At the Naumburg Bandshell, of course!

How did Bow Bridge get its name?

The shape of this bridge is based on an archer's bow.

What is at Central Park's north end?

From 86th Street north, check out the Jacqueline Kennedy Onassis Reservoir, the Conservatory Garden, the Charles A. Dana Discovery Center, and Central Park's oldest building, Blockhouse No. 1.

Where can you find the Mad Hatter and Cheshire Cat?

Along with Alice, they're at the *Alice in Wonderland* statue.

What sits on top of each Central Park lamp post?

An acorn.

Is there only one kind of bench in Central Park?

There are four.

Credits

Author **Fran Quittel** is a native New Yorker who, since 1996, has split her time between the Bay Area and 57th Street in Manhattan, at the foot of Central Park. *The Central Park Lost Mitten Party* was inspired by a visit to the Brooklyn Academy of Music, where Fran's adopted "almost aunt" Florence dropped one glove. "Don't worry about that glove," Fran said. "It's in Central Park having a party!", to which "Aunt" Florence replied, "Now that's all right in a story for children!" Fran has a B.A. from Hunter College and an M.Phil. from Yale University.

Illustrator **Salma Arastu** is a painter, sculptor, print maker, and calligrapher. Her delightful paintings, drawings, and sculptures celebrate energy, form, color, and movement.

Ukrainian-born **Anastasia Podvysotska** now lives in Northern California. Anastasia drew the characters of Molly and her mother, as well as their home and Central Park backgrounds. She is studying to be an architect.

Graphic designer **Paul Veres** is a retired high school art teacher and an award winning font designer. His typeface, Caterina, was chosen by HarperCollins for the cover of *Go Set a Watchman*, the sequel to *To Kill a Mockingbird*.

Linda Gordon, Reader-in-Chief, is based in Eugene, OR, and has happily applied her critical eye and proof-reading skills to a wide variety of manuscripts.

How did Bow Bridge get its name?

Where can you find the
Mad Hatter and Cheshire Cat?

What is at Central Park's
north end?